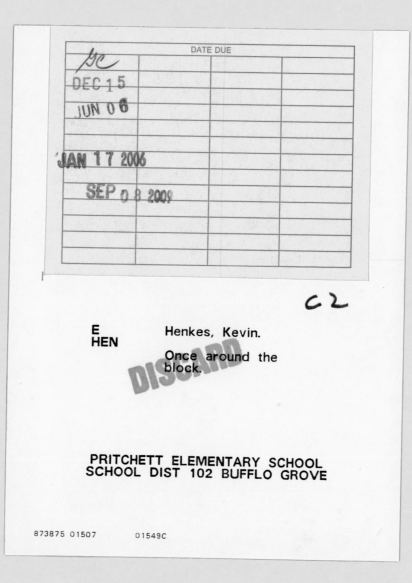

ONCE AROUND THE BLOCK

pictures by Victoria Chess

KEVIN HENKES

Once
Around
the
Block

 GREENWILLOW BOOKS, NEW YORK

The full-color paintings were done in watercolor and ink.
The typeface used is ITC Caslon No. 224.

Library of Congress Cataloging-in-Publication Data
Henkes, Kevin.   Once around the block.
Summary: Annie is bored until a walk around the block to
visit her neighbors brings several pleasant diversions.
[1. Boredom—Fiction.   2. Neighborliness—Fiction]
I. Chess, Victoria, ill.   II. Title.
PZ7.H3890n 1986   [E]   85-24901
ISBN 0-688-04954-0   ISBN 0-688-04955-9 (lib. bdg.)

FOR KELLY—YOUR VERY OWN BOOK

Annie's best friend Bea was on vacation. Mama was busy with baby Phil. Cornelius had fleas. And there was nothing good on television. So Annie sat on the front steps waiting for Papa to come home from work.

"What's the matter, Annie?" Mama called between Phil's screams.
"There is absolutely nothing to do," said Annie. "And I've been
waiting for Papa to come home from work for *hours*."
"Papa will be home soon," said Mama. "But to make the time go by
faster, why don't you take a little walk? Once around the block."

Annie jumped down the steps and turned left.

She walked to Mr. Stewart's house.

Mr. Stewart was sprinkling his front lawn.

"Hello, Miss Sunshine," he said. "Why are you so smiley?"

"Because," said Annie, "my best friend Bea is on vacation. Mama is busy with baby Phil. Cornelius has fleas. There's nothing good on television. And I've been waiting for Papa to come home from work for *hours*."

"Why don't you take your shoes off and run your toes through my grass?" said Mr. Stewart.

The grass was short and soft and green and thick.
And it felt good between Annie's toes.
"Thank you," said Annie. She put her shoes back
on and continued down the street.

Annie walked past the Carters' house, the Clinkenbeards' house, and
the Martins' house. She turned the corner and stopped at Miss Potter's.
Miss Potter was rocking back and forth in her rocking chair.
The chair creaked then stopped, creaked then stopped.

"Hello, dear," she said. "Beautiful afternoon, isn't it?"

"Not really," said Annie. "My best friend Bea is on vacation. Mama is busy with baby
Phil. Cornelius has fleas. There's nothing good on television. And I've been waiting
for Papa to come home from work for *hours*."

"How about two warm chocolate chip cookies, then?" said Miss Potter. The cookies
were larger than Annie's hand and were loaded with melting chocolate chips.

"Thank you," said Annie.

She ate one cookie, put the other in her pocket for later,
and continued down the street.

Annie walked past the Trentons' house, the Mills' house, and the Lesters' house. She turned the corner and stopped at Mrs. Douglas's.

Mrs. Douglas was crouching in her garden, using a small trowel to dig up dirt around her flowers.

"Hello, Annie," she said. "This weather is just right for my petunias and roses and daisies."

"But not for me," said Annie. "My best friend Bea is on vacation. Mama is busy with baby Phil. Cornelius has fleas. There's nothing good on television. And I've been waiting for Papa to come home from work for *hours*."

"Would a pretty rose cheer you up?" said Mrs. Douglas.

The rose was just beginning to open, the petals folding back.
"Thank you," said Annie. She smelled the rose and carefully
held it as she continued down the street.

Annie walked past the Taylors' house, the Welchs' house, and the Shepards' house. She turned the corner and stopped at the big mailbox. Barney the mailman was locking up the box for the night.

"Hello, Annie," he said. "You just have to sing on a day like today."
"Not me," said Annie. "My best friend Bea is on vacation. Mama is busy
 with baby Phil. Cornelius has fleas. There's nothing good on television.
 And I've been waiting for Papa to come home from work for *hours*."
"Want to jingle my keys while I rest a minute?" said Barney.

The keys were large and heavy, and they made nice music.
"Thank you," said Annie. She gave the keys one last jingle
and she started singing as she continued down the street.

Annie walked past the Barritts' house, the Smiths' house,
and the Madisons' house. She turned the corner and stopped
at Bea's. The house was empty and dark.

Annie kept walking. Before she knew it, she was in front of her
own house. And Papa was sitting on the front steps.

"Annie!" he called. "Where have you been? Mama's busy with
baby Phil. Cornelius has fleas. There's nothing good on
television. *And* I've been waiting for you for *hours*."

Annie gave the cookie to Papa.

She gave the rose to Mama.

She jingled Papa's keys for baby Phil.

And after dinner she ran her toes
through the grass while the sun set.